Bear in Trouble

Written by Jill Eggleton

Illustrated by Jim Storey

Rigby

This is a story about...

Bear

Big Bird

The place in the book

the cave

Bear put his head out of the cave.
There was snow on the ground.

"Snow looks good," said Bear.
"I'm not staying
in this cave to sleep.
That's boring.
I'm going out!"

Bear went out into the snow.
Snow fell on his head.
His feet made holes in the snow.
Bear liked it.
Big Bird came flying down.

"Get back!
Get back to your cave.
You can't be out in the snow."

But Bear said,
"I am out in the snow and I like it.
Caves are boring."

Bear will...

stay in the snow?

go back to
his cave?

Bear walked on in the snow.
Then he stopped.

He had a cold head.

He had a cold tail.

He had cold feet.

"I'm going back to my cave now," said Bear.

Bear will...

get back to the cave?

stay in the snow?

Bear looked back.
Where was his cave?
He walked back in the snow.
He was cold all over.

Bear shouted at the sky,
"Where is my cave?"

And the sky shouted back,
"My cave, my cave!"

Bear was shivering!
His tail was shivering!
His ears were shivering!
He was shivering all over.

"I will have to make
a cave in this snow," said Bear.

So he made a big hole in the snow and he laid down.

Bear is...?

But the snow came down
on top of Bear.
It went in his ears.
It went in his eyes.
It went in his mouth!
He was shivering
and shivering!

Bear shouted at the sky,
"Where is my cave?"

And the sky shouted back,
"My cave, my cave!"

Then down from the sky
came Big Bird.
He flapped his big wings
over Bear.

"Come with me.
Come with me.
I will take you back."

Bear got up.
Big Bird was flying
over the snow.
So Bear went with him.
Big Bird took Bear
back to his cave.

"Your cave.
Your cave," said Big Bird.
"Stay here, stay here!"

"Thank you, thank you,"
said Bear.

Bear is...?

Bear went into the cave.
It looked good.
It looked warm.

"I'll stay here,"
he shouted to Big Bird.

Big Bird was gone,
but the sky shouted back,
"Stay here, stay here!"

Bear did.
He stayed in his cave
all winter, and
it wasn't boring at all!

Maps

Bear's Trail

Big Bird went back to the cave...
this way? — · — · — · — —
this way? — — — — —
this way? · · · · · · · · ·

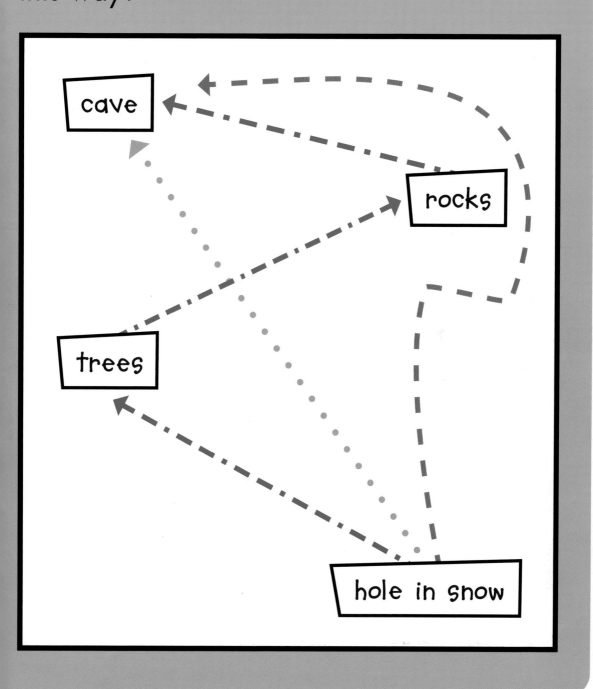

Word Bank

cave

head

ears

mouth

eyes

snow

feet

tail